❧ Simon Solitude ❧

A Story Told in Stories

Words by: **Danny Bakhshi**

Pictures by: **Lex Plotnikoff**

Grosvenor House
Publishing Limited

This book is published by
Grosvenor House Publishing Ltd
28-30 High Street, Guildford, Surrey, GU1 3HY.
www.grosvenorhousepublishing.co.uk

A CIP record for this book
is available from the British Library

ISBN 978-1-906210-92-2

To those who believe

And

To those who mock

Thanks to

Melanie, Julie and of course Lex

Anti-perspirant

Feverishly Simon sprayed his bedroom walls with anti-perspirant. He covered the walls twice, making sure every square inch had been sprayed. That night he went to sleep smiling, secure in the knowledge that his bedroom walls would not sweat during the night.

Spinning

If I could just find a single point of stillness, a place where time and space have stopped spinning, where silence lives. I am always tripping, always falling but never landing. I just need a single instance of stillness - a place where thoughts are frozen and nothing moves, a place where I can regain my balance. Then everything would be fine and I would be ok.

Identity

If half the people in the World could give
identities and the other half could take them....

A man comes up to me
And he takes away my identity,
So now he is me.
Another man approaches he who is now me
And gives him a different identity.
Where am I? What has happened to me?

Angles

Sometimes Simon wakes up and he finds there are too many or too few angles in the world. On days where he fears there are too many angles – days of high angular flux – Simon walks turning this way and that to get through as many degrees as he can, to use up as many angles as he can. And on days where angular flux is low, Simon does his best to conserve degrees and save angles by staying absolutely still. Silly Simon Solitude.

Overcast Eyes

On an overcast day Simon fell in love with a girl with overcast eyes.

Simon and the Sea

When Simon was six years old his mother would prepare a packed lunch for him to take to school. But every day, instead of going to school, Simon would walk down to the local beach and spend the day throwing his packed lunch, crumb by crumb, into the sea. Soon the school sent a truancy officer around to Simon's home. Simon's parents were shocked and concerned to hear of Simon's truancy.

"Simon, why aren't you going to school? Has something happened? Are you alright? We are very worried about you."

"Mum, Dad, you don't understand," Simon replied, "I have to feed the Sea."

People

There are so many people inside me.
Imagine a forest with thousands of trees,
Each tree has a thousand boughs. Can you see?
Each bough has a thousand leaves
And each leaf is me.
There are so many people inside me.

Satan

When Simon was a baby Satan came and pissed in his ear.

Screaming

Why was she screaming? I held her tightly in my arms but she would not stop screaming, screaming, screaming.

The People of Personality

Simon wrote down all the different personalities he felt lived inside his body. He called them the People of Personality. He listed them all down and then tore up the list into a thousand pieces which he took outside and threw into the air. He watched as the pieces of his personality flew away in the wind like confetti.

Inverted Time

Invert geometry.

Invert space and time.

Invert mathematics.

Invert One.

Invert I.

Do you know that time is relative?

Do you know that time fluctuates?

It does, it fluctuates.

The Cherry Tree

Simon Solitude grew a cherry tree. And the cherries on his cherry tree were the skies, brightly overcast. And as Simon ate the cherries he ate her brightly overcast eyes.

Thunder and Lightening

Sometimes the rubble on the hard shoulder of the motorway is made out of thunder and lightening.

Laughter

Can you hear the laughter?
Do you recognize yourself?
Tell me,

Do the others laugh too?
Do they laugh at the things you laugh at?
Or do they laugh at you?

Simon and The Wolf

The first time Simon cried wolf nobody believed him and the wolf ate him up in one gulp.

The Dark

Do not be afraid of the dark, little girl. The dark is not going to hurt you. Be afraid of what is hiding in the dark.

Jigsaw Mum

Simon's mum is a jigsaw puzzle. She is a lady painted onto the surface of an egg. The egg has been broken and the pieces of eggshell are the pieces of Simon's mum

Giraffe

I met a lady with a giraffe's neck. She has a normal enough body and a normal enough head but her neck is a giraffe's neck. I asked her why she had a giraffe's neck but her ears were too high up to hear me. I shouted up at her but she was too busy chewing leaves off a tree to answer me.

Eggshell Skin

The girl Simon loved had skin so delicate it resembled eggshell. Her skin was so fragile that once, when Simon pushed her over, she fell to the floor and her skin shattered into a million pieces.

Betrayal

I ran out into the hallway. I was two or three steps from the door when I sensed her behind me, standing on the stairs. I turned around – he had followed me out. Fool. She was staring at him from the staircase but he had not seen her. I pointed to her. There. She is there. He turned towards her as she fired the gun. The sound of the gunshot ricocheted around the hall, bouncing off the walls and inside, around my head. His body fell backwards back through the doorway. I looked up at her. She began to cry. Not for him or for herself but because I had betrayed her.

The Violin Sea

I saw six hundred thousand hands floating on a violin sea.

Each held a bow and their music was blue and green.

The violins parted and she came to me.

I reached out, swam out, to meet her

But she was gone and six hundred thousand hands pulled

me down.

I drowned in the violin sea.

Silent Echoes

"Do sounds have shadows?" she asked me. I don't know. Do words have flavour? I thought to myself. "Sounds do have shadows," she continued, "Silent echoes are the shadows of sounds." Silent echoes – I whispered the words and savoured their taste

Halo

Today I found a halo lying in the street. Maybe somebody dropped it. Maybe it fell from the sky. It was not mine anyway so I left it and walked past.

Sun Shine

When Simon was five, his mum would give him a packed lunch to take to school. He would have a couple of sandwiches, a packet of crisps, some fruit and three coconut biscuits. Always three coconut biscuits. They were Simon's favourite biscuit.

One day Simon decided during his morning break to have a coconut biscuit. He often did this during his morning break. There was nothing out of the ordinary about his decision to have one early. And later that day at lunch time, after his sandwiches and his apple and his crisps he ate the last two coconut biscuits. They were good. As usual.

Later, during the afternoon break, Simon regretted having eaten the last two biscuits at lunch time. He wished he had had the foresight to only have one and to leave one for later, for now. He opened his lunch box to see if he could catch a trace of coconut biscuit smell. It would be better than nothing. To his astonishment there was a whole coconut biscuit still in his lunch box! There were only three biscuits in his lunch box that morning at morning break and there had been only two at lunch time and he had eaten them both. But here was a fourth coconut biscuit. Somehow it had appeared between the end of lunch time and now!

Ever since that day when the sun has been shining it has shined on Simon.

Dali's Moustache

Sometimes when Simon wakes up in the morning he sees that the shoelaces on his perfect shoes are actually Salvador Dali's moustache.

Blue

Sailing on a sea of Blue electricity
I meet a spark - it ignites me!
Blue Flames scorch my soul
And the spark leaps into my eye.

Conversation

"Be scared. There are people in this World without souls, they suck the souls out of other people and consume them. And the longer one stays in their company, the less soul one has. Soon these people will rule the Earth and no one with a soul will be left alive. And everything beautiful about humanity will have gone forever."

"For every ounce of human kindness, there is a man whose acts are mindless."

"But he knows he can convince you he is superior in race."

Rio

Are things as real and as vivid as they seem? Reality fell apart at the seams today and waterfalls came pouring through, I saw them. In my mind I live in Rio.

Simon and the Elephants

Simon sat at the highest window of the keep, surveying the plain stretched out before him. He heard the rumble of the elephants' stampede before he saw them. They came over the crest of the distant hills and quickly began crossing the plain towards him. Simon watched until they had reached the foot of the keep. He got up and went to look for his gun.

When Simon returned to the window, he saw that one of the elephants – a naked fair haired young man – was climbing the wall of the keep. Without hesitating Simon leant out of the window and shot him. Then he shot the rest of the elephants.

Eggshell Girl Descriptions

Sultry, Eggshell Girl, you are looking sultry.
Voluptuous, you are the gratification of my senses.

Smouldering, your eyes are burning without flames.

A vamp, you bitch, you are a vamp!

Words

A bird that acts mad catches fish.
I cannot open the door anymore.
Words. Just words.

Tiny Feet

The minute men are coming. They are small, aren't they? They are in fact minute. Minute men. Be careful lest they walk all over you with their tiny feet.

Moses

Moses came by the other day. He is considering shaving off his beard and his moustache. I have warned him that it will harm the public's perception of him as a prophet. He has ignored me and gone ahead and shaved. You cannot tell anyone anything these days. How the hell can Moses be clean shaven?

The Beatles and the Rolling Stones

She has poetic feet the colour of a summer's day. And her toes can each play a different musical instrument. And boy, they are good! Her toes are the Beatles and the Rolling Stones!

Drop

A nightingale with a broken heart sang a song full of broken notes. One of the notes floated to the ground and splashed there like a drop in a puddle.

Little Bo Peep

Wherever he went the radiators flocked after him. He was like Little Bo Peep for those radiator sheep.

More Eggshell Girl Descriptions

Eggshell girl you need a bath

Eggshell girl you smell of stale sweat

Eggshell girl you are a bimbo.

Eggshell girl VOMIT

Eggshell girl! Stop wobbling your head!

You Knew

Hey Mr Piston, don't you tread on my toes.

Hey Mr Pneumatic drill, don't play on my knees.

Hey there Piston, you have broken my nose!

And you Pnu, you knew.

You always knew.

Cancer

I went to the amusement park with her sister and her. I told her I was too scared to go on the rides and she said she did not like me smoking cigarettes. Her sister stole my money and I am still having nightmares over the rides. And she has cancer.

Horse

The man with the mane and the horse's teeth is in fact a horse.

Anti-perspirant Returned

He woke up slowly, lingering in the twilight time between dreams and reality. Daylight streaked into the room through his bedroom window. Simon opened his eyes and turned his face away from the light. The wall he now faced glistened where streaks of light landed. Hesitantly he reached out and touched the wall. It was wet.

His bedroom walls had sweat during the night.

A Pertinent Question

"Well, I have to agree. It is a particularly pertinent question" he said as Satan pissed in his ear."

Polaris

She talks about bubblegum and nail varnish but her voice is napalm over the jungles of Vietnam and I remember the other day when she was a Polaris missile erupting from its silo.

Elbows and Hands

My friends where are you?
The room is full of elbows and hands.
Where have you all gone?

Egg With an Eye

A man with a single long eye and no body hair. An oval shaped man. An egg with an eye.

Nufs

People eat pears
A4, lined and margined pears
Pears made of dice

People eat peaches
Granite, crossword peaches
Peaches you can play like pianos

And people eat Nufs
And without knowing it
They eat themselves

Nuit

Fish

The fish have teeth. Sharp, menacing teeth. They are snapping their jaws and I can see cold hatred in their eyes. They are lined up on one side of the ground waiting and snapping their jaws. The ground begins to tilt. Oh no. I know where this is going. The ground begins to tilt and I know pretty soon I will lose my balance and fall down the slope towards the fish. I look down at the fish. They look hungry.

Heart

Sometimes the beat of his heart is the only proof he has that time has not stood still.

Roses

Is this the Feast of Roses?
Is there anyone you would die for? Maybe one.
Where is your mercy now?

Two Questions

Does she laugh with her eyes closed?
And is her laughter the sound of a river?

Manifesto

Each word is a brush stroke, each sentence a flavour.
If you cannot draw form then concentrate on colour.
This manifesto is full of good advice for the talent-
less but it won't get you elected

∽ Simon Solitude ∾

A Story Told in Stories.

I hope you enjoy my painting.